EGMONT
We bring stories to life

First published in Great Britain 2015 by Egmont UK Limited
The Yellow Building, 1 Nicholas Road, London W11 4AN

Written by Emil Fortune
Designed by Richie Hull
Illustrated by Robert Ball

© & ™ 2015 Lucasfilm Ltd.
ISBN 978 1 4052 7895 9
60816/1

Printed in Italy

To find more great *Star Wars* books, visit www.egmont.co.uk/starwars

EPISODE IV:
A NEW HOPE

IT IS A PERIOD OF CIVIL WAR. REBEL
SPACESHIPS, STRIKING FROM A HIDDEN
BASE, HAVE WON THEIR FIRST VICTORY
AGAINST THE EVIL GALACTIC EMPIRE.

DURING THE BATTLE, REBEL SPIES MANAGED
TO STEAL SECRET PLANS TO THE EMPIRE'S
ULTIMATE WEAPON, THE DEATH STAR, AN
ARMOURED SPACE STATION WITH ENOUGH
POWER TO DESTROY AN ENTIRE PLANET.

PURSUED BY THE EMPIRE'S SINISTER
AGENTS, PRINCESS LEIA RACES HOME
ABOARD HER STARSHIP, CUSTODIAN OF THE
STOLEN PLANS THAT CAN SAVE HER PEOPLE
AND RESTORE FREEDOM TO THE GALAXY...

SECRET MESSAGE

As Imperial soldiers take over her ship, Princess Leia Organa, the young senator from Alderaan, hides the Death Star plans in her faithful droid R2-D2. Use the key below to translate her secret message.

HELP ME OBI WAN
KENOBI YOU'RE
MY ONLY HOPE

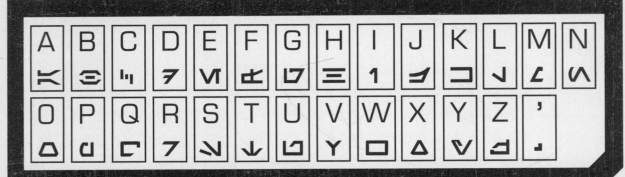

A	B	C	D	E	F	G	H	I	J	K	L	M	N

O	P	Q	R	S	T	U	V	W	X	Y	Z	'

LORD **VADER**

Leia has been captured by the Empire's sinister Sith Lord, Darth Vader, who draws his power from the dark side of the Force. Can you change DARK to SIDE, changing only one letter at a time?

D A R K

~~D~~	~~i~~	~~r~~	~~k~~
B	A	R	E
H	I	R	E

S I D E

CLUES:
skin of a tree
wearing nothing
the cost of a journey
shoot
give someone a job
conceal

DROID DESIGNER

R2-D2 and his counterpart C-3PO escape Darth Vader – but their escape pod crash-lands on the desert planet Tatooine. They are captured by Jawas, who sell all kinds of scavenged droids – design your own using the blueprint page opposite.

R4-E1

R5-D4

R2-D2

POWER DROID

REPAIR **R2-D2**

R2-D2 and C-3PO have been bought by Luke Skywalker's Uncle Owen and Aunt Beru to work on their farm. Luke needs to fix R2-D2 – can you work out which of the microchips below matches this one?

1.

Xf'sf eppnfe!

We're doomed!

2.

Uijt jt bmm zpvs gbvmu.

_____

3.

Tfdsfu njttjpo? Xibu qmbot?

_____

4.

J'n hpjoh up sfhsfu uijt.

_____
_____

PUZZLE
PROTOCOL

C-3PO is a protocol droid – he knows six million languages! But his translation circuits are scrambled. Every letter in these quotes is one later in the alphabet than it should be – shift them back to work out what he's saying. The first one is done for you...

DESERT DASH

Following Leia's secret orders, R2-D2 has run away to find 'Old Ben' Kenobi, who lives in the Dune Sea. Guide Luke's speeder through the desert maze to find them. Look out for the Tusken Raiders!

START HERE

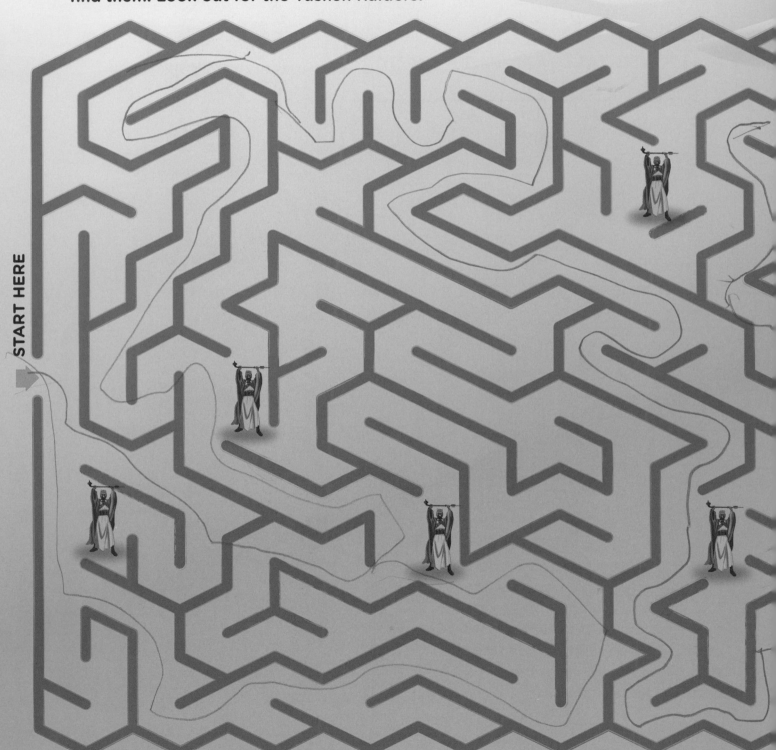

FINISH!

OBI-WAN SUDOKU

The Sand People ambush Luke, but Ben Kenobi saves him. Ben reveals that his name is really Obi-Wan Kenobi. Luke's father, like Obi-Wan, was a Jedi Knight who fought in the Clone Wars.

Obi-Wan wants Luke to come with him to Alderaan, to deliver the Death Star plans – and so Luke can train in the ways of the Force.

Can you solve this Obi-Wan Sudoku? Write the letters O, B, I, W, A and N in the grid so that there is only one of each letter in each row, column, and 2x3 box.

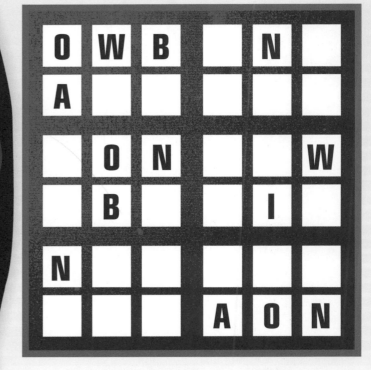

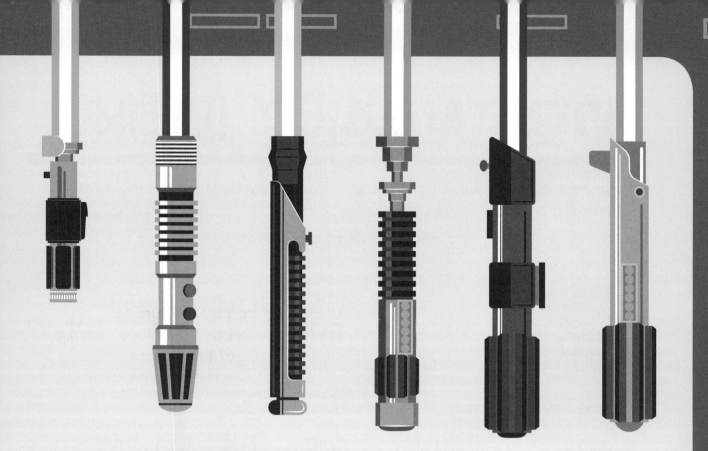

LIGHTSABER LINEUP

The lightsaber is the weapon of the Jedi Knights – they used them to duel villains like the evil Sith Lords. What would yours look like? Draw your ideal lightsaber below.

MOS EISLEY MENU

Luke and Obi-Wan have come to the Mos Eisley Cantina hoping to find a ship and a pilot to take them to Alderaan.

Solve the riddle to find out what drink Luke orders at the bar.

My first is in **BLASTER** and also in **PUB**

My second's in **SOLO** and also in **CLUB**

My third is in **DUEL** but never in **BLADE**

My fourth's in **IDEA** but never in **AID**

My fifth is in **EMPIRE** and also in **MAUL**

My sixth is in **WIRED** and also **INSTALL**

My seventh's in **LEIA** but not in **ADMIRE**

My last's in **KENOBI** but not in **BONFIRE**

Write the answer here:

ALIEN ALLIES

The Cantina is full of weird and wonderful aliens from all over the galaxy. Draw your own strange creature here and give it a name.

RODIAN

DUROS

DEVARONIAN

NAME:

UNUSUAL SUSPECTS

A Rodian called Greedo has been shot at the Mos Eisley Cantina. Write down the highlighted clues in the order that they are numbered to find out who did it.

CLUE 1

CLUE 6

Greedo's gun was out of its holster.

He said something to the human. I think it was a threat.

I'm sure I heard two pistols fire.

CLUE 4

CLUE 3

I heard Greedo was a bounty hunter.

CLUE 5

I saw a human leave the Cantina in a hurry.

I didn't see anything. I just heard a blaster.

CLUE 2

I saw a Rodian sit down at the table.

CLUE 7

ENTER YOUR CLUES HERE, THEN READ THE RED COLUMN

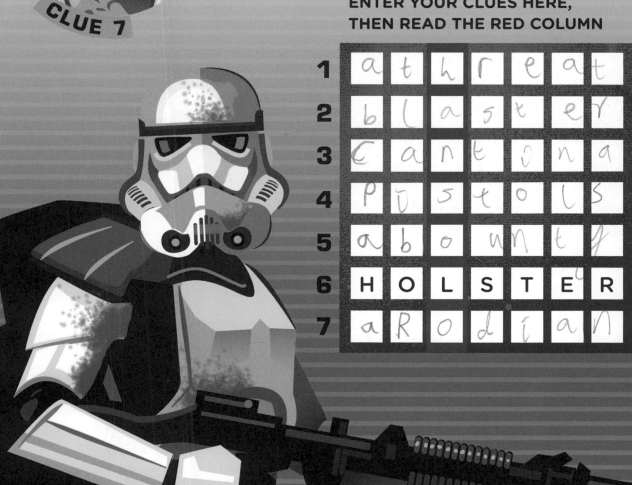

#						
1	a	t	h	r	e	a	t
2	b	l	a	s	t	e	r
3	c	a	n	t	i	n	a
4	p	i	s	t	o	l	s
5	a	b	o	u	n	t	y
6	H	O	L	S	T	E	R
7	a	R	O	d	i	a	n

JUMP START

A smuggler, Han Solo, agrees to take Luke, Obi-Wan, and the droids to Alderaan on his starship the *Millennium Falcon*. With Imperial forces closing in on them, can you help set the navigation computer so they can jump to lightspeed? What is the missing symbol from the readout above?

WOOKIEE WARNING

Han Solo's co-pilot Chewbacca, a fierce Wookiee, likes Holochess. Solve the code below to find out the best strategy for playing against him.

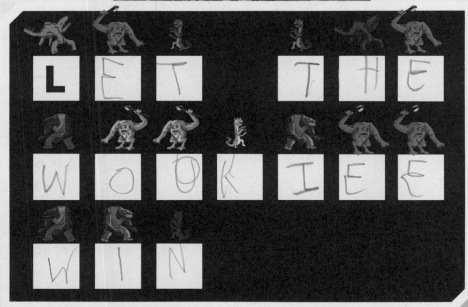

LET THE
WOOKIEE
WIN

TROOPER TEST

Han and Luke have disguised themselves as stormtroopers to infiltrate the Death Star. Can you work out which two troopers they are? All the others are identical.

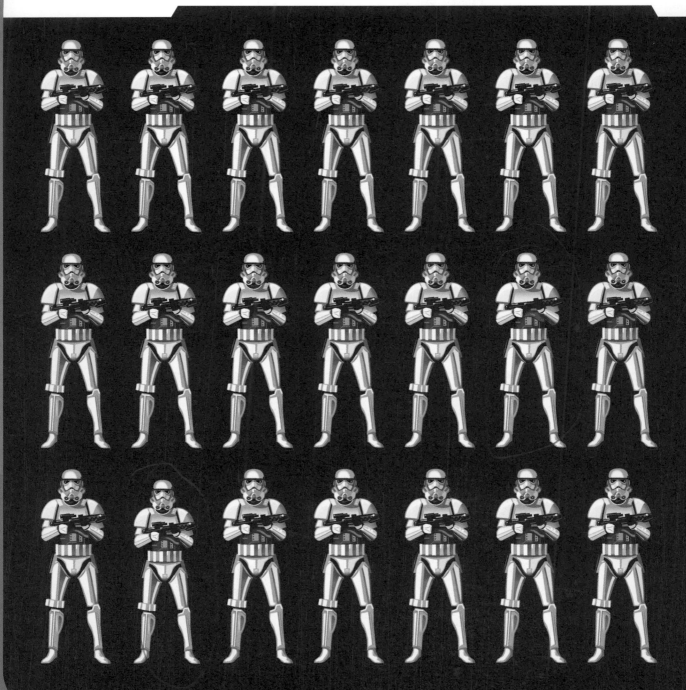

TRACTOR BEAM CHALLENGE

Obi-Wan must reach the tractor beam controls so that they can escape when they have completed their mission. Help him make his way through the Death Star's corridors, avoiding the stormtrooper patrols.

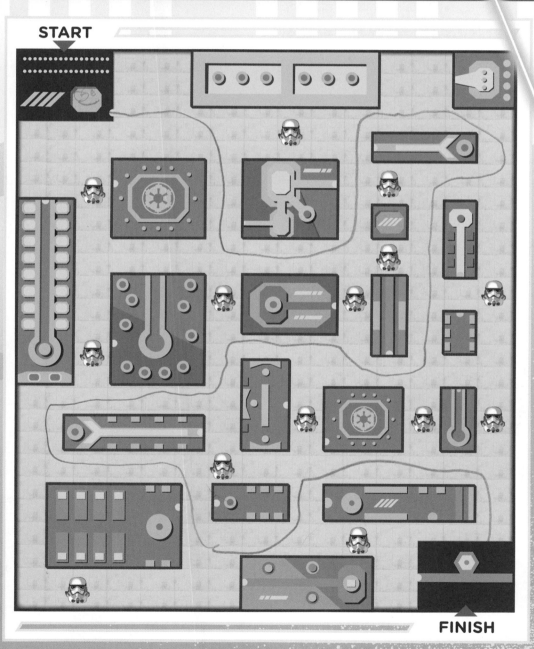

START

FINISH

DEATH STAR
DOWNLOAD

R2-D2 plugs into the Death Star's computer. "He should be able to interpret the entire Imperial network from here," says Obi-Wan. Help him find his way through the system to where Princess Leia is being held.

START

SECURITY SCRAMBLE

Solve the anagram to unlock the prison door.

NEPO LELC CKLOB

TARKIN'S TARGET

The commander of the Death Star, Grand Moff Wilhuff Tarkin, is holding Leia prisoner. He wants the location of the Rebel Base. Cross out every other letter to find the name of the decoy planet Leia reveals – and the planet Tarkin destroys instead.

D~~X~~ALNETAO
QOSIWNVE

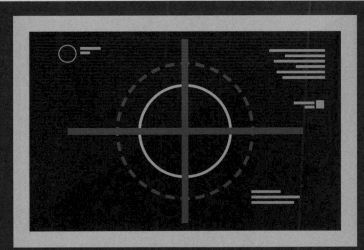

ANLXDJEU
RSAPAON

The Empire's spies are everywhere. Garindan has intercepted the following images, but parts of them are missing. Use the stickers to add characters to the scenes.

This Jawa sandcrawler brought the droids to a moisture farm run by Owen Lars. Add some droids to the scene to complete the lineup.

The droids were tracked to Mos Eisley spaceport – a dangerous place! Add some aliens, bounty hunters and droids to the scene. And who are the stormtroopers questioning?

JEDI TRAINING

"You must learn the ways of the Force, if you're to come with me to Alderaan," says Obi-Wan. How much do you know about *Star Wars*? We have started you off with two answers – all the others are in this book.

ACROSS

4,7	Owner of the *Millennium Falcon* (3,4)
5	Desert bandits (4,6)
7	See 4 across
13	C-3PO's droid companion (5)
14	Tarkin's rank (5,4)
16	Imperial starfighter (3)
18	____ Vader (5)
19	Greedo, for example (6)
20	Married to Luke's aunt Beru (4,4)
22	A battle between two people (4)
23	The guardians of peace and justice in the galaxy (4)
24	Rebel fighter (1-4)
25	Imperial spy (8)

DOWN

1	Where Darth Vader draws his power from (4,4)
2	Episode IV's title (1,3,4)
3	Princess Leia's government position (7)
6	Married to Luke's uncle (4,4)
7	Han Solo's job
8	Obi-Wan and Luke's father fought together in the … (5,4)
9	Tusken ____ (6)
10	Where the secret Death Star plans must be taken (8)
11	C-3PO, for example (5)
12	Desert beast, ridden by 5 (6)
15	Luke's home (4)
17	Desert hermit (3,3)
20	Ben's real name
21	The Senator from Alderaan (4)
23	Desert scavenger (4)

12 B
13 A R T O O
A N
16 T H A
A

TRASH TROUBLE

Luke and his friends have managed to rescue Princess Leia – but now they are trapped in a garbage masher with slimy monsters! Which monster has got hold of Luke?

MASHER MAYHEM

As the walls of the garbage masher close in, Luke makes a desperate call to C-3PO. Can you find all the words below in the grid?

G	B	T	H	R	E	E	P	I	O	L
L	A	C	C	A	G	E	I	B	H	T
D	A	R	H	U	N	E	J	X	U	N
E	I	L	B	E	S	S	O	K	W	K
T	Q	C	Q	A	W	L	O	O	R	S
E	D	U	E	T	G	B	D	L	R	V
N	X	O	U	E	L	E	A	E	O	L
T	N	H	K	E	B	G	H	C	A	E
I	S	U	V	Z	U	S	W	X	C	I
O	L	E	Z	G	A	R	T	O	O	A
N	L	M	G	M	V	F	S	V	Z	T

FIND THESE WORDS!

THREEPIO	SHUT
ARTOO	DOWN
HAN SOLO	GARBAGE
LUKE	MASHERS
LEIA	DETENTION
CHEWBACCA	LEVEL

FIGHTER FLIGHT

Having escaped the Death Star, the crew of the *Millennium Falcon* are chased by Imperial TIE fighters. Copy the TIE Advanced into the targeting grid to fight them off.

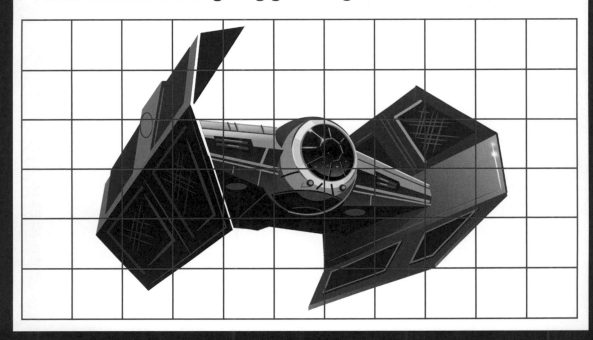

TRACKER TRICK

The *Millennium Falcon* is on its way to the Rebel Base with Princess Leia – but Vader has hidden a tracking device on the ship. Use the grid to copy the tracker readout below.

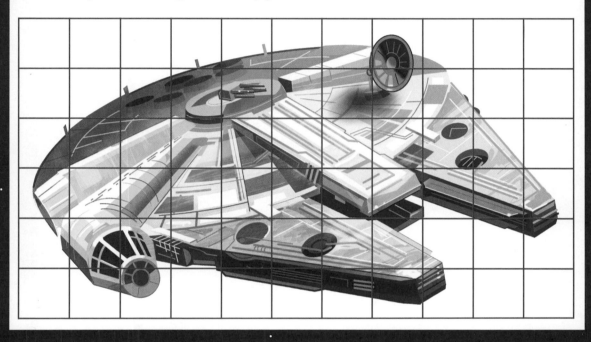

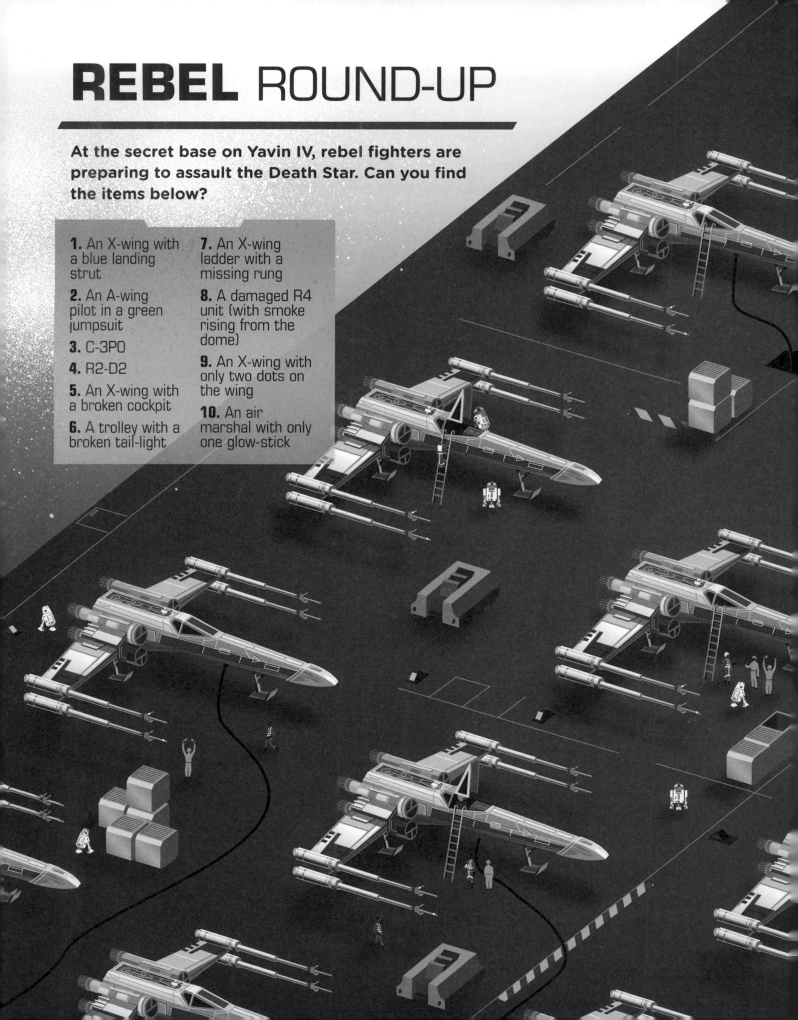

REBEL ROUND-UP

At the secret base on Yavin IV, rebel fighters are preparing to assault the Death Star. Can you find the items below?

1. An X-wing with a blue landing strut

2. An A-wing pilot in a green jumpsuit

3. C-3PO

4. R2-D2

5. An X-wing with a broken cockpit

6. A trolley with a broken tail-light

7. An X-wing ladder with a missing rung

8. A damaged R4 unit (with smoke rising from the dome)

9. An X-wing with only two dots on the wing

10. An air marshal with only one glow-stick

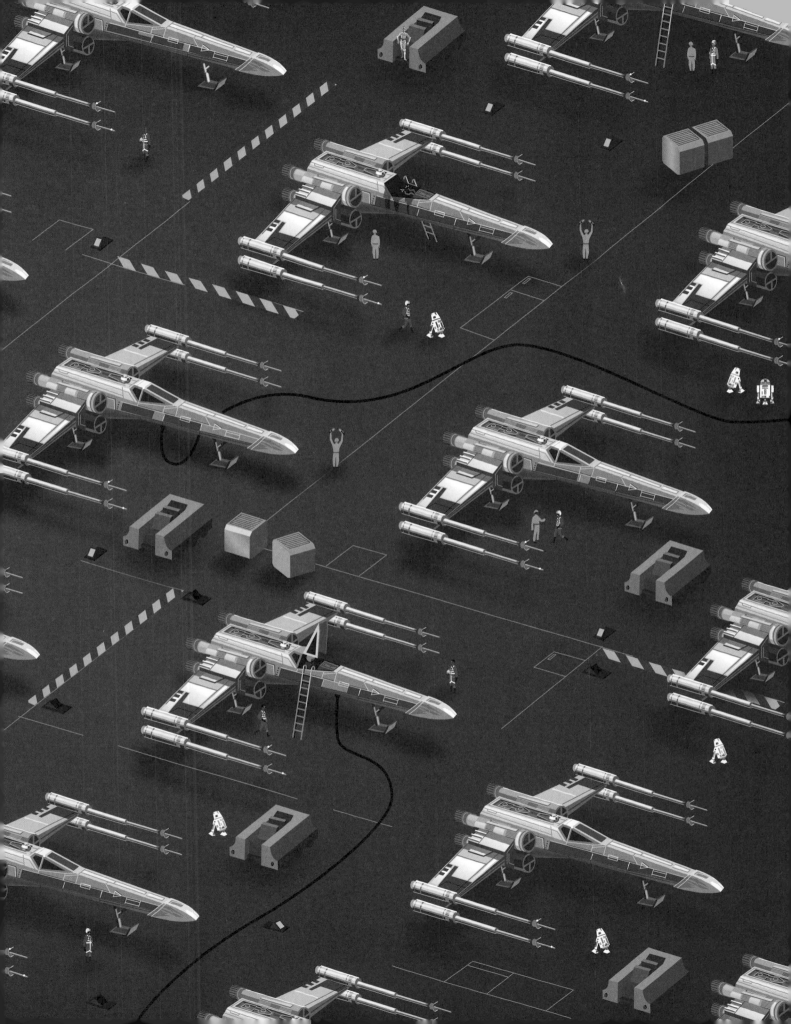

RED SQUADRON

Luke joins the fighter pilots of Red Squadron. Can you match these pilots to their callsigns by unscrambling the clues?

RED 2:
TEENAGED WILLS

RED 3:
BRIGHT RAGGED SILK

RED 5:
WREAK SKULL KEY

RED 6:
PROTON SINK JOKE

WEDGE ANTILLES ▼

RED 2

RED 3

RED 5

RED 6

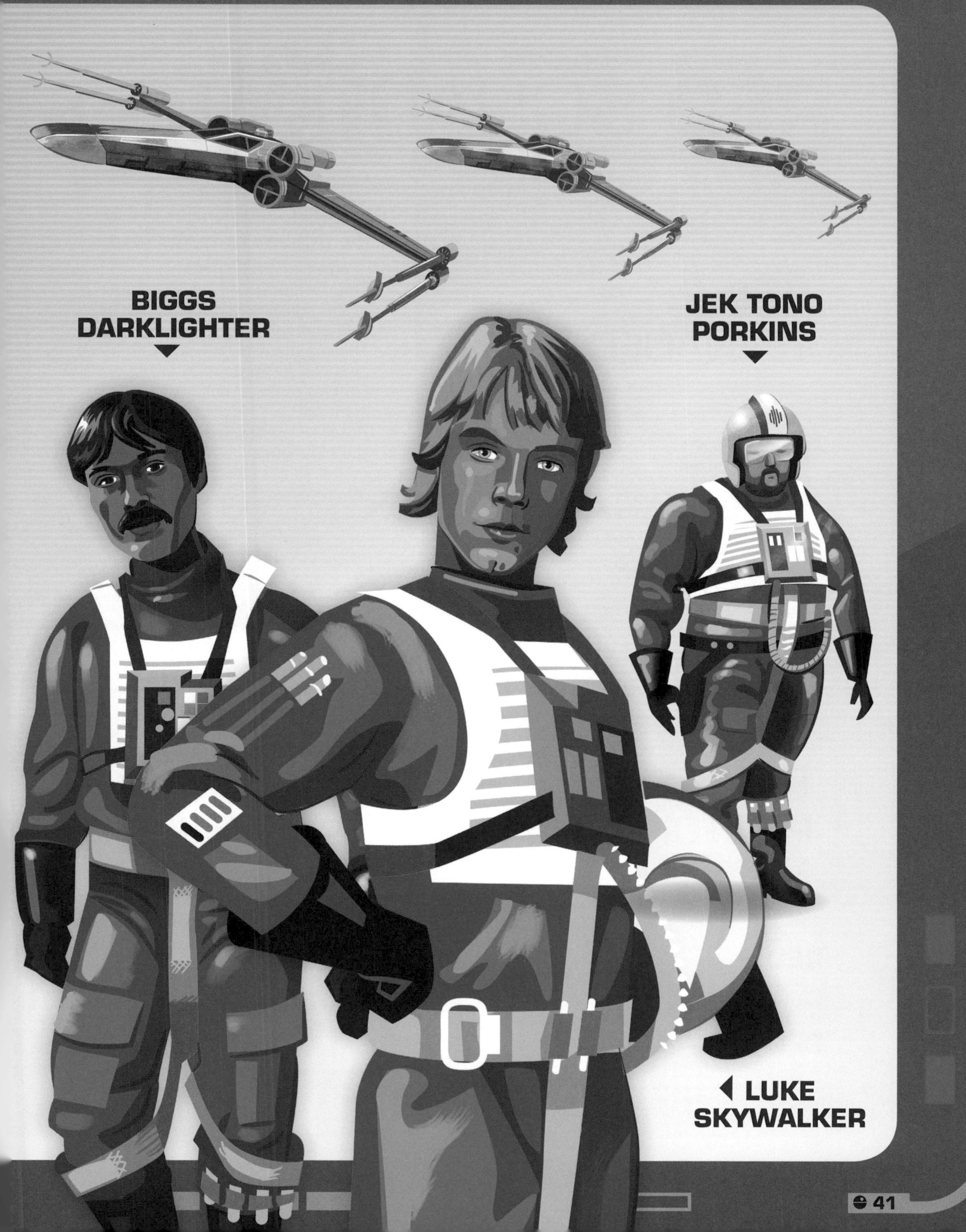

BIGGS
DARKLIGHTER
▼

JEK TONO
PORKINS
▼

◀ LUKE
SKYWALKER

SPACE BATTLE!

The attack begins! Fill the rest of the fighters in to the grid, following these rules:

- There must be an equal number of TIE fighters and X-wings in each row and column
- There cannot be three TIE fighters or three X-wings in an unbroken line
- No two rows or columns can be identical
- Practice on the easy grids, then try the hard ones!

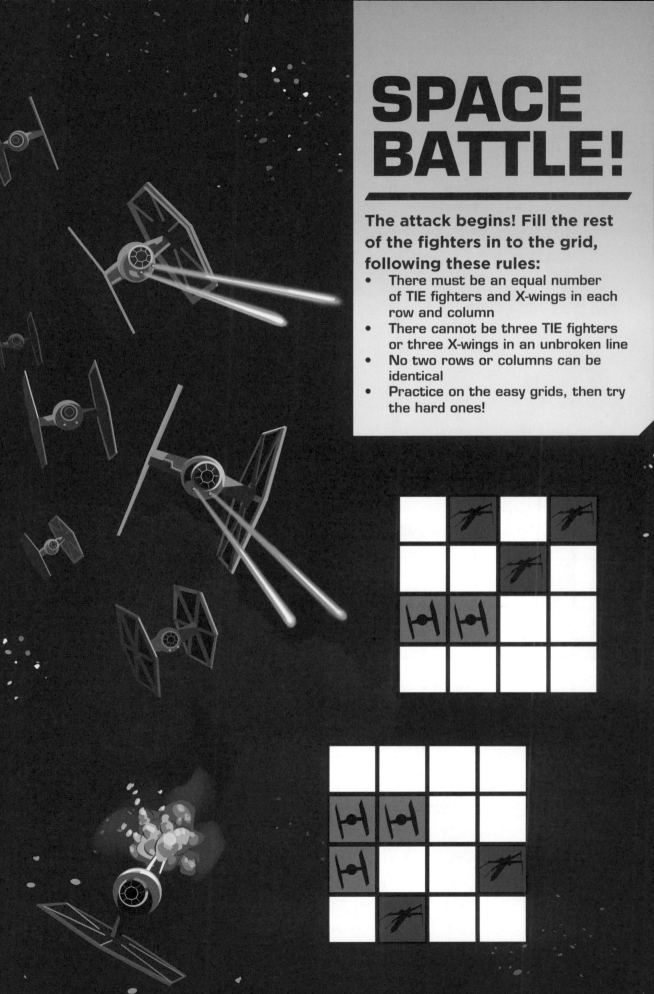

INSTRUCTIONS

Red Squadron must make it past the Imperial defenses and through the Death Star trench to hit the thermal exhaust port. One player is the REBEL player, and one is the IMPERIAL player – use coins or buttons for markers. Roll one die each to see who goes first. Each turn, roll one die to move, and follow any instructions on the squares. The first player to the finish line wins.

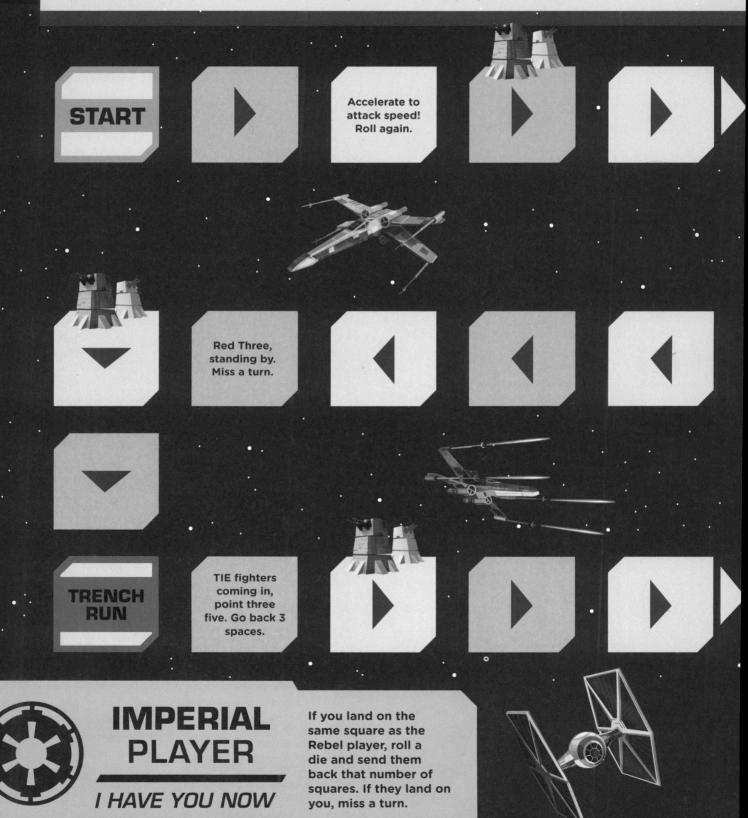

START

Accelerate to attack speed! Roll again.

Red Three, standing by. Miss a turn.

TRENCH RUN

TIE fighters coming in, point three five. Go back 3 spaces.

IMPERIAL PLAYER

I HAVE YOU NOW

If you land on the same square as the Rebel player, roll a die and send them back that number of squares. If they land on you, miss a turn.

REBEL PLAYER

USE THE FORCE!

Before you throw the die, you may guess which number you will roll. If you are right, move twice the distance. If you are wrong, move one space only.

Engine hit! Miss a turn while your astromech repairs it.

S-foils to attack position! Go forward 2 spaces.

You're too low – pull up! Go back one space.

Stay in attack formation. Go forward 3 spaces.

Just like Beggar's Canyon back home! Roll again.

You must roll the exact number needed to land on this square. If it is too high, go back to TRENCH RUN

FINISH

FINAL FORCE

Luke must use the Force to guide a proton torpedo into the Death Star's thermal exhaust port. Using everything he has learned, fit the following words into the grid. One has been added in to get you started.

Ben Kenobi
Alderaan
Lightsaber
Chewbacca
Leia Organa
Wilhuff Tarkin
Republic
Fighters
Rebels
Han Solo
A New Hope

CONGRATULATIONS!

The Death Star has been destroyed.
Design a medal to commemorate this famous victory!

ANSWERS

Page 4:
HELP ME OBI WAN KENOBI
YOU'RE MY ONLY HOPE

Page 5:
bark
bare
fare
fire
hire
hide

Page 6:
C

Page 7:
1. We're doomed!
2. This is all your fault.
3. Secret message? What plans?
4. I'm going to regret this.

Page 10-11:

Page 12:

O	W	B	I	N	A
A	N	I	O	W	B
I	O	N	B	A	W
W	B	A	N	I	O
N	A	O	W	B	I
B	I	W	A	O	N

Page 13:
F

Page 14:
BLUE MILK

Page 16-17:
HAN SOLO

Page 18:

Page 19:
LET THE WOOKIEE WIN

Page 20:

Page 21:

Page 23:

OPEN CELL BLOCK

Page 24:
DANTOOINE
ALDERAAN

Page 32-33:
1. Dark Side
2. A New Hope
3. Senator
4,7: Han Solo
5: Sand People
6: Aunt Beru
7 down: Smuggler
8: Clone Wars
9: Raider
10: Alderaan
11: Droid
12: Bantha
13: Artoo
14: Grand Moff
15: Farm
16: TIE
17: Old Ben
18: Darth
19: Rodian
20: Owen Lars
20 down: Obi-Wan
21: Leia
22: Duel
23: Jedi
23 down: Jawa
24: X-wing
25: Garindan

Page 34:
B

Page 35:
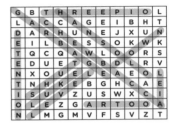

Page 38:
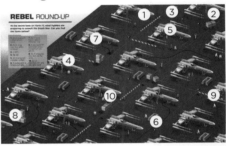

Page 40:
RED 2: Wedge Antilles
RED 3: Biggs Darklighter
RED 5: Luke Skywalker
RED 6: Jek Porkins

Page 42:
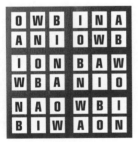

Page 43:

Page 46: